MR. WORRY

by Roger Hargreaves

Grosset & Dunlap
An Imprint of Penguin Random House

Poor Mr. Worry.

Whatever happened, he worried about it.

If it rained, he worried that his roof was going to leak.

If it didn’t rain, he worried that all the plants in his garden were going to die.

If he set off shopping, he worried that the shops would be closed when he got there.

And when the shops weren’t closed when he got there, he worried that he was spending too much money shopping.

And when he got home with his shopping, he worried that he'd left something behind, or that something had fallen out of his basket on the way home.

And when he got home, and discovered that he hadn't left anything behind, and that nothing had fallen out of his basket on the way home, he worried that he'd bought too much.

And then he worried about where to put it all.

Life was just one long worry for poor Mr. Worry.

One day, he went for a walk.

He was worried that he might walk too far and not be able to get home, but on the other hand, he was worried that if he didn't walk far enough, he wouldn't get enough exercise.

He hurried along worrying.

Or you could say, he worried along hurrying.

He met Mr. Bump.

"I'm very worried about you," he said.

“Why’s that?” asked Mr. Bump.

“I’m worried that one of these days you might hurt yourself,” he said.

“Don’t you worry your head about that,” replied Mr. Bump.

And went off.

Tripping over his own feet.

Mr. Worry went on.

He met Mr. Noisy.

"I'm very worried about you," he said.

"Why's that?" asked Mr. Noisy.

"I'm worried that you might lose your voice," said Mr. Worry.

"Don't you worry your head about that," said Mr. Noisy.

And went off.

CLUMP! CLUMP! CLUMP!

Mr. Worry went on.

He met Mr. Greedy.

"I'm very worried about you," he said.

"Why's that?" asked Mr. Greedy.

"I'm worried that you might eat too much and be sick," explained Mr. Worry.

"Me?" replied Mr. Greedy.

"Eat too much?"

"Impossible!"

And went off.

For lunch.

Mr. Worry went on.

He met a wizard.

“Hello,” said the wizard. “Who are you?”

“I’m Mr. Worry.”

“And you look it,” commented the wizard.

“Tell you what,” he went on, for he was a helpful sort of a wizard. “Why don’t you go home and write down every single thing that you’re worried about, and I’ll make sure that none of these things ever happen.”

He smiled.

"And then you won't have anything to worry about, will you?"

Mr. Worry smiled.

It was the first time he'd smiled in a long time.

In fact, it was the first time he'd smiled that year.

He hurried home in great excitement.

When he got home, he sat down to write out all the things that worried him.

Every single thing.

It was a long list!

And then he went to bed and had the best night's sleep he'd had in years.

The following morning, the wizard came round to collect Mr. Worry's list.

"My goodness me," he said when he saw the size of it.

"However," he said, "leave it to me. I'll go off and make sure that none of these things ever happen."

And off he went.

"Nothing to worry about now," he called over his shoulder. "Nothing at all!"

Mr. Worry heaved a sigh of relief.

That day was the first day in Mr. Worry's life that he didn't have a single thing to worry about.

And the next day.

And the day after.

And the day after that.

On Monday, Tuesday, Wednesday, Thursday, Friday, Saturday, and Sunday, Mr. Worry didn't have a care in the world.

But . . .

On Monday morning he was a worried man.

Oh dear.

What do you think was worrying him?

Can you guess?

He went to see the wizard.

"Oh dear," said the wizard when he saw him standing on his doorstep. "What's worrying you?

"I'll tell you," said Mr. Worry.

“I’m worried because I don’t have anything to worry about!”

And he went home.

To worry about not having anything to worry about!